KALYANI NAVYUG MEDIA PVT LTD
New Delhi

Sitting around the Campfire, telling the story, were:

Wordsmith	:	Lewis Helfand
Illustrator	:	Rakesh Kumar
Illustrations Editor	:	Jayshree Das
Colorist	:	Prasanth K. G.
Color Consultant	:	R. C. Prakash
Letterer	:	Bhavnath Chaudhary
Editors	:	Mark Jones Eman Chowdhary
Editor (Informative Content)	:	Pushpanjali Borooah
Production Controller	:	Vishal Sharma

Cover Artists:

Illustrator	:	Rakesh Kumar
Colorist	:	Rajiv Chauhan
Designer	:	Manishi Gupta

Published by Kalyani Navyug Media Pvt Ltd
101 C, Shiv House, Hari Nagar Ashram
New Delhi 110014
India
www.campfire.co.in

ISBN: 978-93-80028-42-2

Printed in India at Rave India

About the Author

Joseph Rudyard Kipling was born in Bombay, India on December 30, 1865. He was the son of Alice MacDonald and John Lockwood Kipling, the latter being a British artist and teacher. In 1871, Rudyard Kipling, as he became better known, was sent to England to live with a foster family. He didn't see his parents for many years.

Kipling's early years spent in India, and the misery and desolation he later felt while in England, provided the inspiration for many of his works. Arguably his best book, *Kim,* is a perfect example of the tremendous impact his personal experiences had on his writing.

After attending the United Services College in North Devon, Kipling returned to India at the age of sixteen to become a journalist. He spent years traveling across the globe while working as a writer, and returned to London in late 1891 due to the death of his friend and collaborator, Wolcott Balestier. Kipling married Wolcott's sister, Caroline, in 1892; and settled in Brattleboro, Vermont shortly after.

While best known as the author of *The Jungle Book,* a collection of stories about a young jungle boy named Mowgli, Kipling's prolific writing career included everything from poetry, to short stories, to novels. *The Light that Failed, Just So Stories, Captains Courageous,* and *Kim* are some of his best-known works.

It is said that he was offered the position of poet laureate, and the honor of a knighthood on at least one occasion. Both of these he declined. Other honors bestowed upon him included a Doctor of Laws degree from McGill University in 1899; the Nobel Prize for Literature in 1907; and a Doctorate of Letters from Oxford in 1907 and from Cambridge in 1908. Rudyard Kipling continued writing until his death on January 18, 1936.

KIM
MOOKERJEE
MAHBUB ALI
THE LAMA
COLONEL
CREIGHTON

Although he spoke the local language, and was on good terms with the small boys of the bazaar, Kim was a white boy—a poor white boy.
In 1901, he was living in Lahore which, at that time, was still a part of India. He stayed with a woman who was not his mother, and she took care of him.
Kim's real mother had been a babysitter. She had married Kimball O'Hara, a young sergeant in an Irish military regiment known as the Mavericks. Kim was named after him.
When Kim's mother died of cholera in Ferozepur, his father turned to drink and then to drugs. He later died from an overdose of opium. This was how Kim became an orphan.
Kim was left with little more than his birth certificate, a certificate that proved his father belonged to the Mavericks regiment, and a prophecy.
The prophecy had been spoken by Kim's father while he was under the influence of opium. He had said that Kim would first see two men making the ground ready...
...then he would see a red bull on a green field and nine hundred devils. And finally, a colonel riding a tall horse would come for him.

One day, young Kim was playing with his friends when he came across a man the likes of whom he had never seen before.
Who are you, old man?
I am a lama—a guru—from the Tibetan hills. What is this big house here? Can I enter it?
It's a museum—the Wonder House! All are free to enter it.
Be careful, strange priests eat boys.
Then run to your mother's lap and be safe!
The lama entered the museum where he was greeted by the curator. Kim followed and hid behind a pillar to listen and watch.
Welcome, Lama. What brings you here from Tibet?
I am looking for a river. Legend says the Lord shot an arrow in a test of strength.
The arrow traveled far and, where it touched the earth, a stream broke out which became a river.
Curious at hearing of the lama's quest, Kim followed him to the curator's office.
I'm sorry, there is nothing here at the museum that would help you find this river. Are you searching for it on your own, or is someone with you?
I did have a disciple, who traveled with me and begged for my dinner, but he died of fever.
I am now returning to my temple in Benares, but I hope to find the river on my way.
I must find that river; I was told in a dream to find it.
When the lama realized the Wonder House could not help him, he left feeling lonely and still no closer to finding the river.

Tired, the lama decided to sit and meditate as to what he would do next.
Do not sit under that gun!
The lama will sit under the gun if it pleases him!
Lama, please forgive this policeman's bad manners, and allow me to beg for your dinner.
Saying that, Kim ran toward the market.
Yes, rice is good, but this is for a holy man!
Give me fish and curry, cake and--
Kim, you are far too bold!
The lama was more than satisfied with what Kim had managed to collect.
Eat now and rest.
A hearty meal and exhaustion soon sent the lama into deep slumber.
ZZZZZZZ
When the lama woke up, he could not see Kim. He worried at the thought of losing his new disciple.
My new disciple! Where are you?
I am over here!
I will accompany you to Benares in the morning. We will look for your river and the bull from my father's prophecy.
But tonight, we should stay at the Kashmir Serai* with a friend of mine.
*The name of an inn.

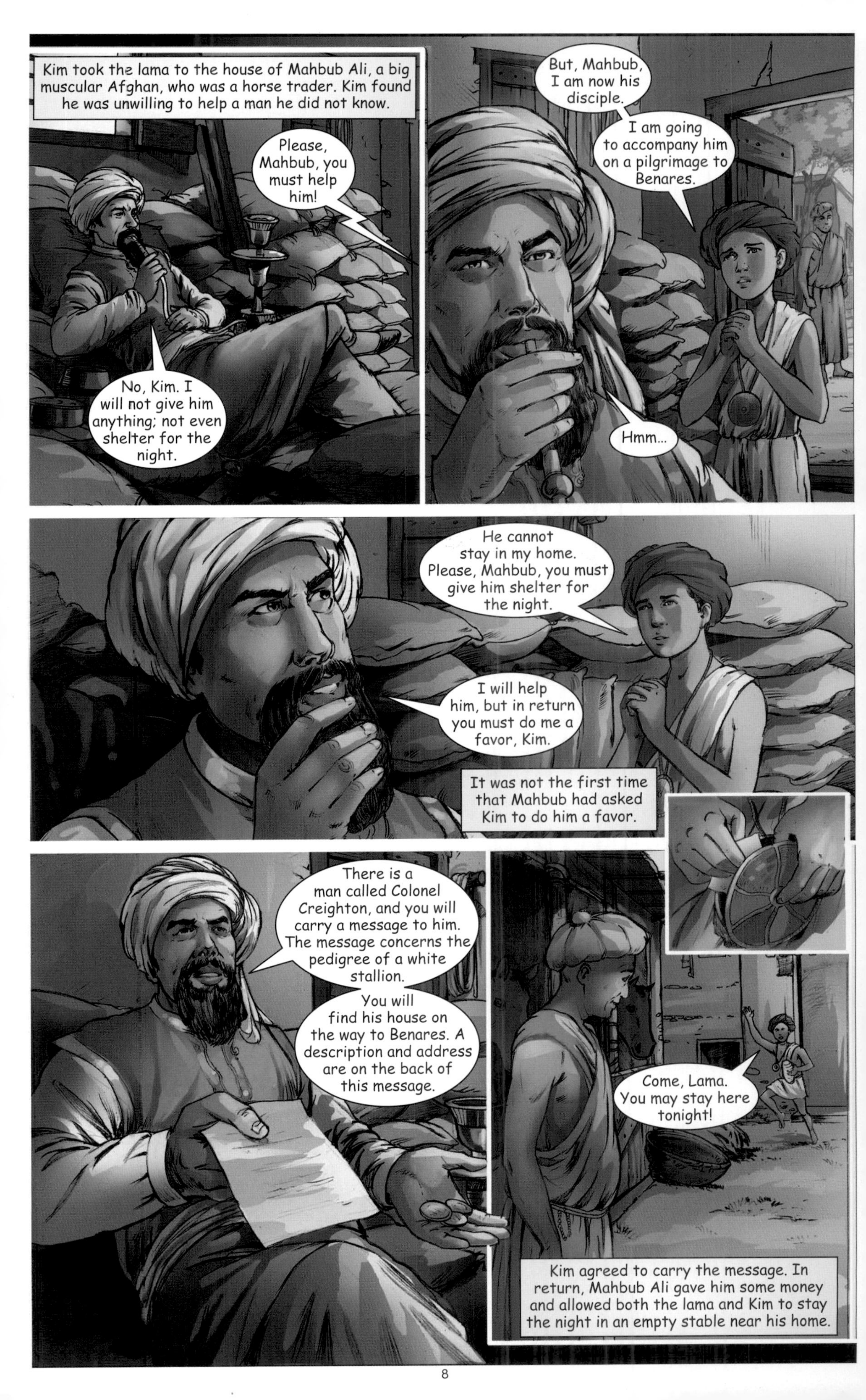
Kim took the lama to the house of Mahbub Ali, a big muscular Afghan, who was a horse trader. Kim found he was unwilling to help a man he did not know.
Please, Mahbub, you must help him!
No, Kim. I will not give him anything; not even shelter for the night.
But, Mahbub, I am now his disciple.
I am going to accompany him on a pilgrimage to Benares.
Hmm...
He cannot stay in my home. Please, Mahbub, you must give him shelter for the night.
I will help him, but in return you must do me a favor, Kim.
It was not the first time that Mahbub had asked Kim to do him a favor.
There is a man called Colonel Creighton, and you will carry a message to him. The message concerns the pedigree of a white stallion.
You will find his house on the way to Benares. A description and address are on the back of this message.
Come, Lama. You may stay here tonight!
Kim agreed to carry the message. In return, Mahbub Ali gave him some money and allowed both the lama and Kim to stay the night in an empty stable near his home.

That night, Mahbub Ali went to a local bar for a drink. He did not know he had been followed or that his drink had been drugged.
He may have sent it away by now.
As soon as he fell unconscious, the man who had put the drug in his drink went to work. He searched Mahbub Ali for a letter that his superiors wanted.
I doubt he had the time. We must find that letter.
When he could not find the letter in Mahbub Ali's pockets, the man then searched his home and stables.
Where has he put it?
He was so intent on finding what he wanted, that he took a knife to everything Mahbub Ali owned.
Perhaps he placed it in the soles of his slippers.
Common thieves don't cut up slippers. This man must want the message Mahbub gave to me.
Come. It is time...
...time to go to Benares.
Kim had known Mahbub Ali for many years, but was unaware that he was known to the British Secret Service as Agent C25.

The two of them rushed to the railway station.
One to Ambala, and one to Amritsar.
As soon as the train left Lahore station, Kim revealed his plan to the lama.
I will save our money. The price of two tickets to Ambala is too expensive.
But I will make sure we both get to Ambala.
Kim's antics did not work on the ticket inspector.
...but I asked for two tickets to Ambala!
Your ticket is to Amritsar only! This stop is Amritsar, and you must get off the train now!
I swear I am telling the truth!
I paid for two tickets to Ambala!
A likely story.
Have you no heart?
Here, my child, buy yourself a ticket to Ambala.
Thank you so much!
Kim's trick, and the pity of a woman, had saved him and the lama a lot of money.

Kim and the lama continued their journey to Ambala. On the way, the lama engaged himself in conversation with another passenger.
You say you seek a river?
Yes, a river of healing.
We live in Ambala. Perhaps you and your disciple would like to stay with us for the night?
Yes, thank you.
After reaching the woman's house, Kim left to deliver Mahbub's message to the English colonel, but kept his intentions secret.
I will be back soon; I am going to try and beg for our dinner.
Checking that he still had the message, Kim remembered what Mahbub Ali had told him...
...that the message concerned the pedigree of a white stallion.
Kim did not believe that was the real intention of the message. He thought about the other favors he had done for Mahbub Ali.
Some of these had included following people all day and telling Mahbub how they had spent their time.

Mahbub Ali's directions brought Kim to the house of the Englishman in Ambala. From the way Mahbub had described him, Kim soon knew which man was Colonel Creighton.
Do not turn around. I have been sent by Mahbub Ali.
And what does Mahbub have to say?
The pedigree of the white stallion is fully established.
He has given me this letter as proof. It is for you. Take it.
Here's a rupee for you. Now get out of here, and quick!

Kim stayed though, long enough to see the Englishman return to the house, and enter a small office.
Will! It seems Mahbub Ali is a man of his word, after all.
Yes, Will. It is war. I'd been expecting it, but this message confirms it.
Yes, Mahbub Ali is a good agent. But, Colonel Creighton, are you sure his message means war?
Then we must respond by sending an army to prevent it.
After Kim had listened in to the colonel's conversation, he headed to the kitchen to see if he could get food and more information.
You seem to be serving a very large dinner. I came to wash dishes in return for a bellyful.
You may help us. But remember, the dinner is in honor of the commander-in-chief, so you must behave yourself at all times.
Kim spent a little time there and, when he had gained some information, went back to the lama.
So the message concerned a war, and the two men said they would send a great army to stop it. What is Mahbub Ali involved in?

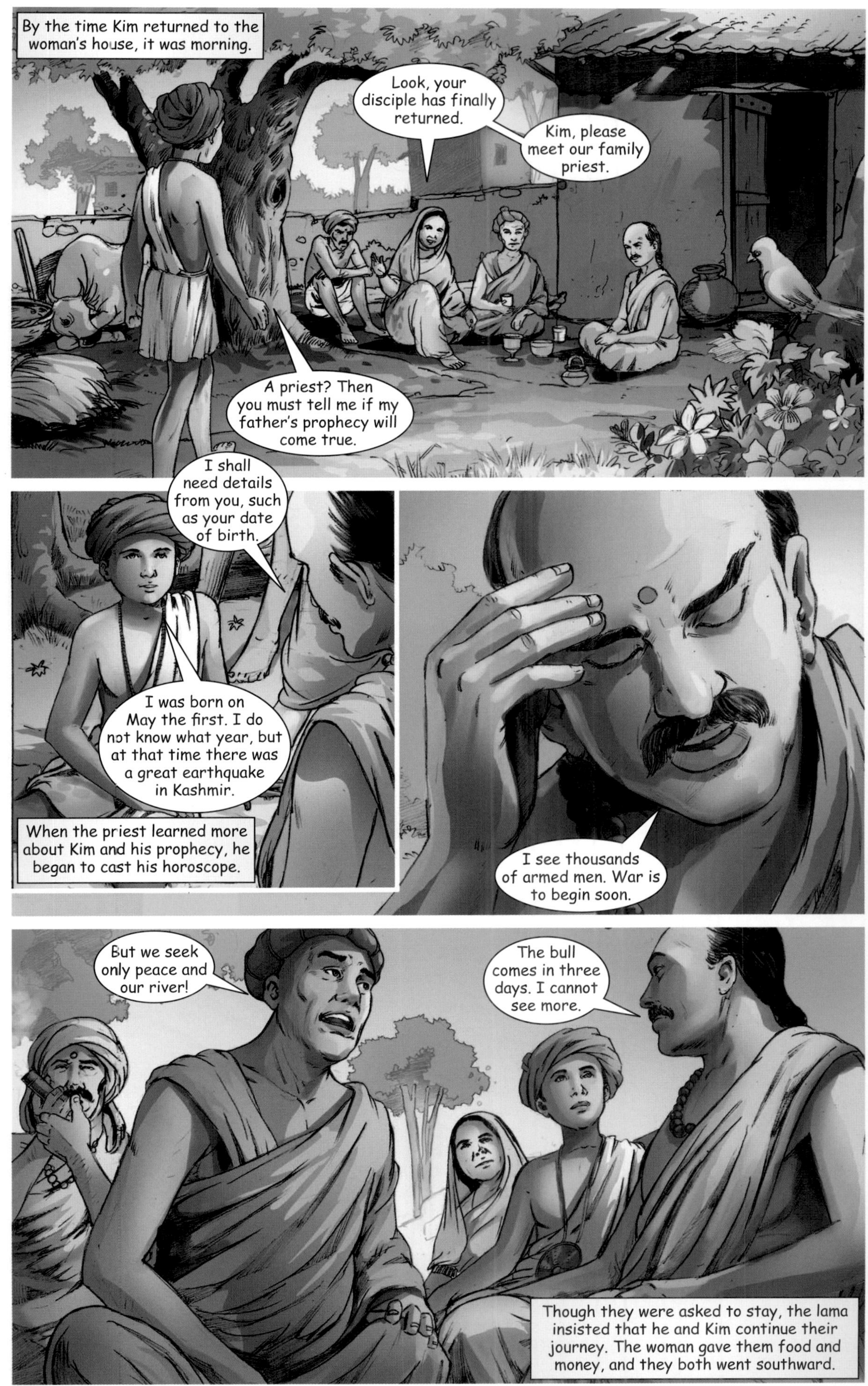
By the time Kim returned to the woman's house, it was morning.
Look, your disciple has finally returned.
Kim, please meet our family priest.
A priest? Then you must tell me if my father's prophecy will come true.
I shall need details from you, such as your date of birth.
I was born on May the first. I do not know what year, but at that time there was a great earthquake in Kashmir.
When the priest learned more about Kim and his prophecy, he began to cast his horoscope.
I see thousands of armed men. War is to begin soon.
But we seek only peace and our river!
The bull comes in three days. I cannot see more.
Though they were asked to stay, the lama insisted that he and Kim continue their journey. The woman gave them food and money, and they both went southward.

The lama was still intent on finding his river and achieving enlightenment.
As they walked from place to place, they met people who were generous and those who were not.
I shall not offer you food or shelter. There are too many beggars in these lands. Go away!
After two days of walking, Kim and the lama had still not found the river. However, they were drawing nearer to Benares.
On the third day of traveling, they came to a village where the people were very generous. They provided food, shelter and directions.
Stay here for the night, and tomorrow you can travel on the Great Road.
It is six miles to the west and runs to Calcutta and Benares. It crosses many streams; perhaps you will find your river while on the road.

The next morning, as they were leaving, Kim told of the prophecy to another priest, while all those in the village listened.
And a priest explained this prophecy in your horoscope?
Yes. He told me that the prophecy indicates there will be a war soon.
There will always be war; one cannot pretend to predict what always happens.
Kim turned to see an old, withered man, who had served the government as a native officer in a cavalry regiment.
He was well respected in the village, and would regularly dress in his uniform from ancient days. English officials often visited him.
There has not been a war like this before—there will be thousands fighting each other.
My sons are officers. They would have told me if what you say is true.
Give me a sign.
Kim described the Englishman who had talked of war. He told of his appearance, how his voice sounded and how he walked. But it was the name he gave that convinced the old soldier he was telling the truth.
He is a tall man, and his name is Colonel Creighton.

Stop! I know the Englishman you speak of. Has there not been enough bloodshed already? I wish to hear no more of it and I only hope I do not see it either.
Those listening drew long, quivering breaths. They stared at the old soldier and the ragged shape of Kim against the blue sky.
After the discussion was over, and Kim had convinced the old soldier that there was to be a war, they decided to move on.
Can you point us in the direction of the Grand Trunk Road?
Come. I know a shortcut
Your search ends here. There is the road you have been looking for.
I hope it leads you to the place you seek.

The Grand Trunk Road was a wonderful spectacle. It ran straight, stretching for 1,500 miles—such a river of life existed nowhere else in the world.
It was built on an embankment to guard against floods from the foothills. Anyone on that road walked a little higher than the land around it, along a stately corridor, seeing all of India spreading out to the left and right.
Another sight the Grand Trunk Road offered was the mixture and variety of people, each clad in their own distinctive colors of red, blue, pink, white and saffron.

After they had walked along the Grand Trunk Road for most of the day, Kim and the lama came to a resting place. Other travelers, both rich and poor, were also gathered there.
See over there, a rich traveler. I shall beg them for money.
Go away! I will not have beggars bothering my mistress.
Take care, my brother, otherwise I will place a curse on you and your employer.
You insolent pup; I will beat you for that insult!
Kim waited to be beaten, but the punishment did not come.
I-I am saved from a great sin.
A lama, at last.
The presence of the lama had saved Kim from a great deal of pain.

If you know the lama, please ask if he would speak with my mistress.
I am the lama's disciple. I will ask if he will speak with your mistress, once he has eaten.
I will bring food for you both—if you will permit me?
Hmm... you are permitted.
You boy, come here! Who is that lama?
He is the most holy of holy men from Tibet. I am his disciple.
You are no more a disciple than my finger is the pole of this wagon.
I am a king's widow, and not a fool.
You are a bold beggar attached to the holy one for gain.
Do we not all work for gain?
Here is a rupee. Make sure he speaks with me!
When he has eaten, he will speak with you.

When Kim and the lama had eaten, the lama spoke with the king's widow.
What did she ask you?
She wants us to travel with her to Bodhgaya, so that we may pray she has a second grandson.
The next morning, the lama told Kim that he had agreed they would travel with the king's widow for the next few days.
Our roads run together for a while, so we can join her without abandoning our search.
After two days of travel, they were almost at Benares when they decided to rest for the night.
In the early hours of the morning, Kim decided to take a better look at the road ahead.
Kim, where are you going?
To look from above, and I see...
...soldiers. White soldiers!
Kim watched the soldiers for an hour, before deciding to take a closer look at them.

In the light of the morning sun, Kim found that, in the plains just off the Grand Trunk Road, an entire army had set up camp.
This is the spot. Put the officers' tents under the trees.
What are they preparing for?
My father's prophecy. It is as the priest who cast my horoscope said!
Two will make the ground ready...
...and there will be a red bull on a green field. Look!
Make sure the flag is straight.
Kim felt a thrill at seeing the prophecy come true.
MAVERICKS
They must be the nine hundred devils!
But the prospect of war also filled him with dread.
Look! A priest. He will understand our search and--
No! Not now. We must come back at night.

Rather than traveling further with the king's widow, Kim and the lama waited until it was dark. This allowed Kim to take a closer look at the soldiers.
I know a little bit about the customs of white soldiers.
I will be back soon.
Kim had always enjoyed the thrill of danger. Earlier it had been jumping from rooftops in Lahore; now it was sneaking into an army camp.
The soldiers of the Mavericks regiment were conducting their nightly toast, unaware that Kim was watching them.
They must be praying to the bull on the table!
Ouch!
Whoooaaaaa!
Kim had managed to trip up none other than Bennett, the Church of England chaplain of the Mavericks regiment.
My arm! Let go of it!
Were you waiting to sneak up and kill me? Is that it?

We'll put some light on that face of yours. I've been told that murderers like to do their killing in the dark.

It's a boy!
Let go!

What's this? A heathen charm?
In trying to grab hold of him, Bennett pulled Kim's amulet off. It was one of the few things that Kim owned and his most treasured possession.

Give it to me. Give me the papers.
Hmm... so you speak English, do you? Where did you steal this from, boy?
I did not steal it! It is my charm. Give it back to me!
Oh, Father Victor! I am glad you are here.

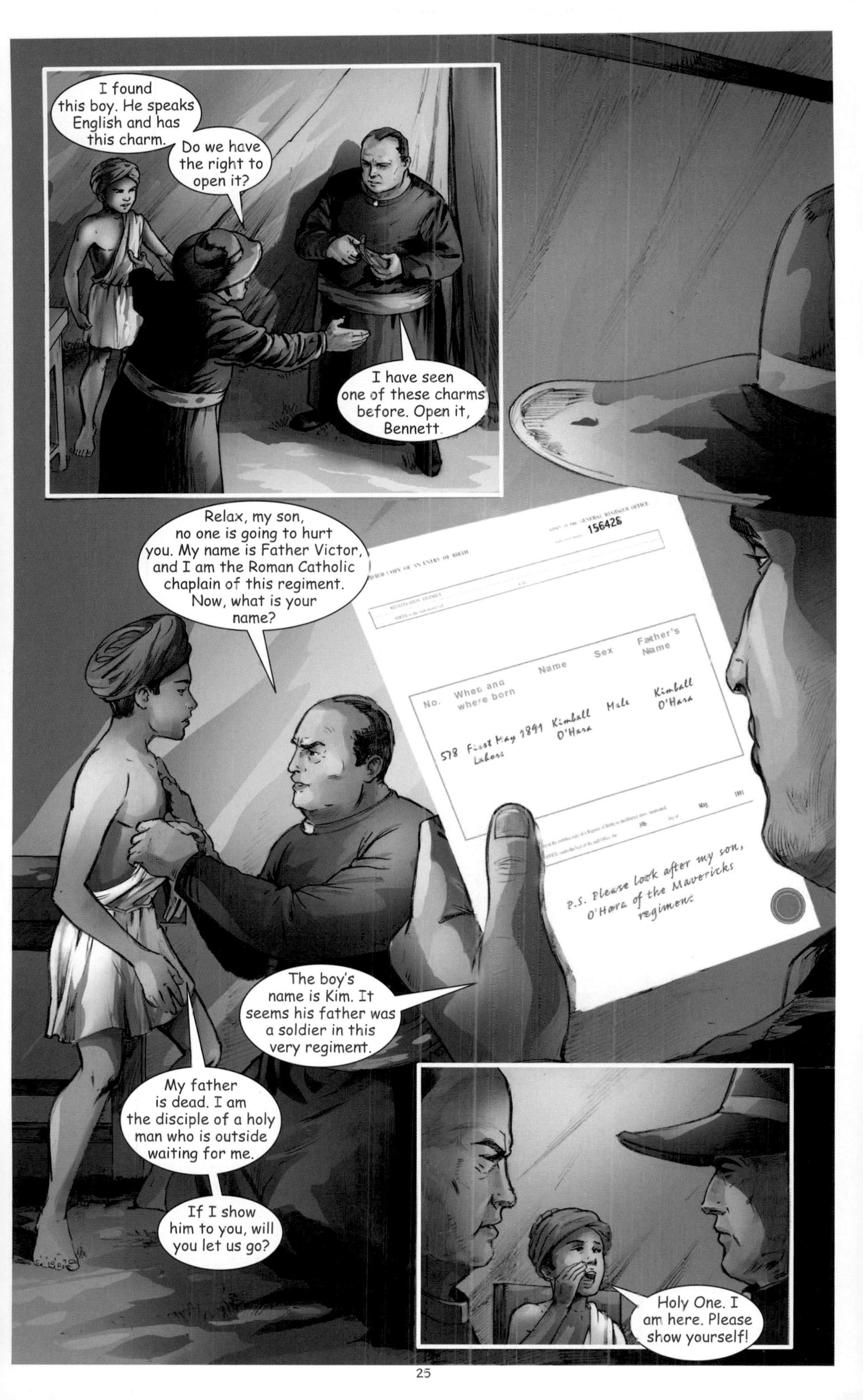
I found this boy. He speaks English and has this charm.
Do we have the right to open it?
I have seen one of these charms before. Open it, Bennett.
Relax, my son, no one is going to hurt you. My name is Father Victor, and I am the Roman Catholic chaplain of this regiment. Now, what is your name?
156428
No.
When and where born
Name
Sex
Father's Name
578 First May 1891 Lahore
Kimball O'Hara
Male
Kimball O'Hara
P.S. Please look after my son, O'Hara of the Mavericks regiment
The boy's name is Kim. It seems his father was a soldier in this very regiment.
My father is dead. I am the disciple of a holy man who is outside waiting for me.
If I show him to you, will you let us go?
Holy One. I am here. Please show yourself!

Have you found what you were seeking, my disciple?
Yes. I found the bull.
His father was a soldier in this very regiment. We can't leave his son to go through life as a beggar!
He must be sent to an orphanage.
Now, Kim, I want you to tell your friend what I say; word for word in a language he will understand.
Holy One, the fool with the hat says that I am the son of a soldier.
Is it true?
Yes, it is true. I have known since birth, but he thinks the son of a soldier should also be a soldier. They will send me to a school.
What are you saying?
If they try to keep me, I will run away and return to you, Holy One.
Please continue your journey to Benares. I will meet you there soon.

Kim knew there was nothing he or the lama could do to stop him from being sent to school. It seemed the lama would have to continue his search for the river alone.
What are you going to do with me?
I will send you to a school first, then you will become a soldier.
I don't want to be a soldier.
If you are to be sent to a school, it should be a good one. Ask them which is the best school and how much it costs.
The lama wants to know the cost of the school.
The best school is in Lucknow, and it costs 300 rupees a year. But you are being sent to a military orphanage, Kim.
Go to the orphanage, Kim. I will send the money for the school in Lucknow soon.
Please give the lama the address of the military orphanage.
He said he will send the money for the better school.
Having said goodbye to the lama, Kim was led away by a sergeant and taken to the military orphanage.
He'll live to thank us.
Come on then, son.

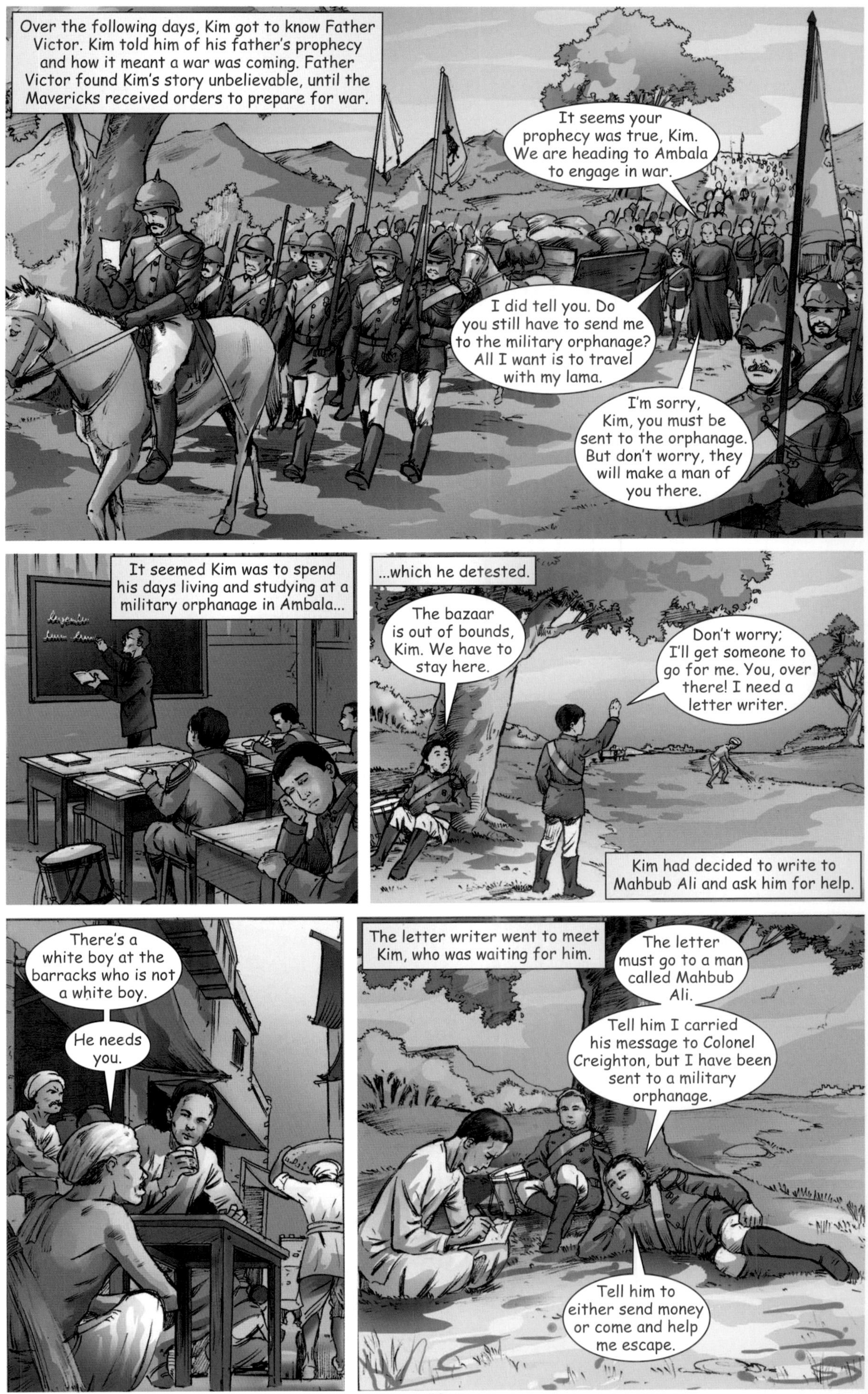
Over the following days, Kim got to know Father Victor. Kim told him of his father's prophecy and how it meant a war was coming. Father Victor found Kim's story unbelievable, until the Mavericks received orders to prepare for war.
It seems your prophecy was true, Kim. We are heading to Ambala to engage in war.
I did tell you. Do you still have to send me to the military orphanage? All I want is to travel with my lama.
I'm sorry, Kim, you must be sent to the orphanage. But don't worry, they will make a man of you there.
It seemed Kim was to spend his days living and studying at a military orphanage in Ambala...
...which he detested.
The bazaar is out of bounds, Kim. We have to stay here.
Don't worry; I'll get someone to go for me. You, over there! I need a letter writer.
Kim had decided to write to Mahbub Ali and ask him for help.
There's a white boy at the barracks who is not a white boy.
He needs you.
The letter writer went to meet Kim, who was waiting for him.
The letter must go to a man called Mahbub Ali.
Tell him I carried his message to Colonel Creighton, but I have been sent to a military orphanage.
Tell him to either send money or come and help me escape.

The next day, Kim was surprised to hear that Father Victor had received a telegram from the lama.
Your lama said that he will send the money for you to be educated at the school in Lucknow. Where did he get the money from, can you tell me that?
I do not know, Father Victor.
I will wait for him to send the payment. If it arrives, you will go to the school in Lucknow.
If not, you will remain here at the orphanage.
Four days later, Father Victor received another letter from the lama, with a banker's note enclosed to pay for Kim's education at Lucknow.
How on earth did the lama get 300 rupees?
Father Victor was lost in his thoughts, when a drummer boy came running in.
He's gone!
Kim O'Hara!
As he rushed to begin looking for Kim, Father Victor began to wonder if it would be more of a relief to find Kim or lose him forever.
A man on horseback took him. He was so quick. He rode in and grabbed O'Hara before anyone could stop him. It was a man with a scarlet beard!
Father Victor couldn't understand Kim and the lama. He spent hours trying to work out how someone he considered to be little more than a street beggar had managed to raise 300 rupees.
RA 35 72186
RA 35 72186
This entitles the bearer to collect THREE HUNDRED Rupees from our branch in Benares.

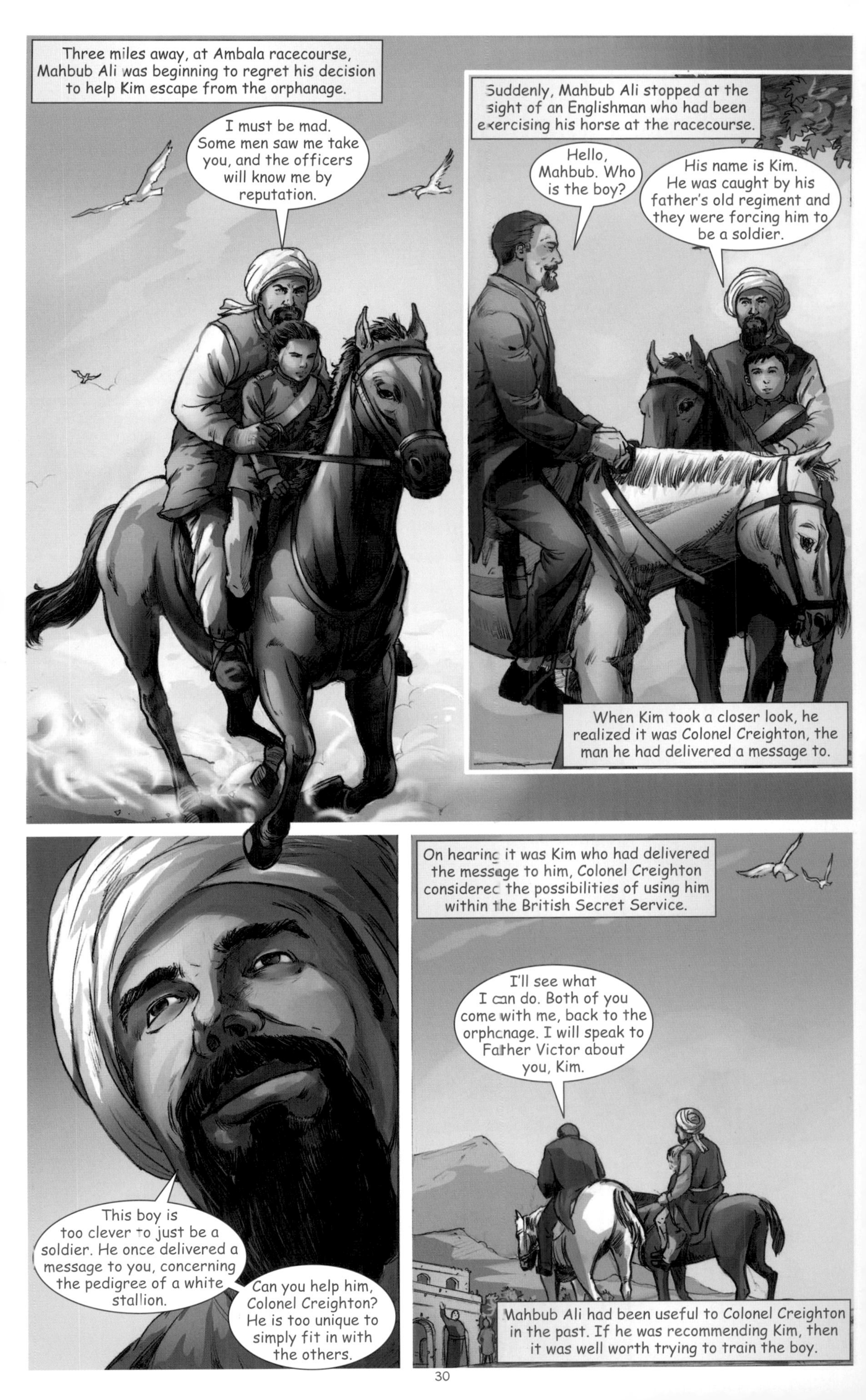
Three miles away, at Ambala racecourse, Mahbub Ali was beginning to regret his decision to help Kim escape from the orphanage.
I must be mad. Some men saw me take you, and the officers will know me by reputation.
Suddenly, Mahbub Ali stopped at the sight of an Englishman who had been exercising his horse at the racecourse.
Hello, Mahbub. Who is the boy?
His name is Kim. He was caught by his father's old regiment and they were forcing him to be a soldier.
When Kim took a closer look, he realized it was Colonel Creighton, the man he had delivered a message to.
This boy is too clever to just be a soldier. He once delivered a message to you, concerning the pedigree of a white stallion.
Can you help him, Colonel Creighton? He is too unique to simply fit in with the others.
On hearing it was Kim who had delivered the message to him, Colonel Creighton considered the possibilities of using him within the British Secret Service.
I'll see what I can do. Both of you come with me, back to the orphanage. I will speak to Father Victor about you, Kim.
Mahbub Ali had been useful to Colonel Creighton in the past. If he was recommending Kim, then it was well worth trying to train the boy.

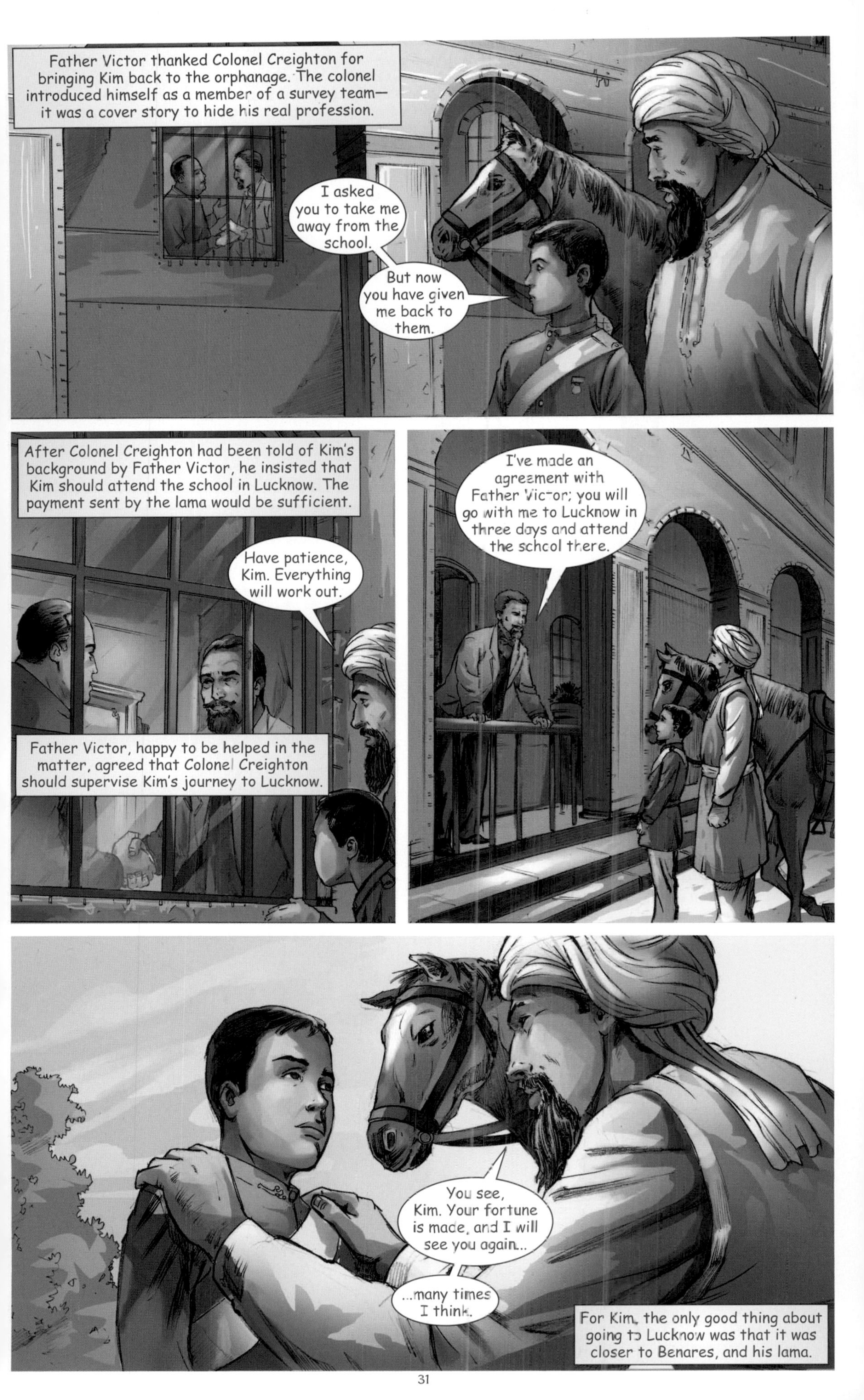
Father Victor thanked Colonel Creighton for bringing Kim back to the orphanage. The colonel introduced himself as a member of a survey team—it was a cover story to hide his real profession.
I asked you to take me away from the school.
But now you have given me back to them.
After Colonel Creighton had been told of Kim's background by Father Victor, he insisted that Kim should attend the school in Lucknow. The payment sent by the lama would be sufficient.
Have patience, Kim. Everything will work out.
Father Victor, happy to be helped in the matter, agreed that Colonel Creighton should supervise Kim's journey to Lucknow.
I've made an agreement with Father Victor; you will go with me to Lucknow in three days and attend the school there.
You see, Kim. Your fortune is made, and I will see you again...
...many times I think.
For Kim, the only good thing about going to Lucknow was that it was closer to Benares, and his lama.

Later that same day, Kim visited the bazaar to pay the letter writer what he was owed, and to ask him to write another letter.
This time I want to send a letter to my lama in Benares, telling him I am going to Lucknow.
Three days later, Father Victor escorted Kim to a second class train carriage bound for Lucknow. Colonel Creighton was also on the same train, but he traveled in the first class carriage.
So, it seems I am to be a soldier after all.
LUCKNO
Now, remember what I told you, Kim.
If you study hard, I will eventually arrange for you to do survey work for me. You will be paid a good wage of 30 rupees a month.
When they arrived at Lucknow station, Colonel Creighton arranged for Kim to be taken to his new school, which was known as St. Xavier's.
Kim felt a great sense of disappointment that the lama was not at the Lucknow train station to greet him. But, on his way to the school, he recognized a familiar face on the street.
Stop!
But we are not inside the school yet.
Just stay here!
I am glad to see you, my lama. My heart has been heavy since we parted.
I received your letter. I have waited here for a day and a half.
How did you get here?

The lama explained that he had not only received a letter from Kim, but also from Father Victor at the orphanage. It told him that Kim would be sent to Lucknow, under the supervision of a man known as Creighton.
ST XAVIER'S LUCKNOW
I traveled here from Benares by train.
I came to make sure the money was paid for your education.
Thank you, Holy One. I have no friends other than you.
I must go now, Kim. I will write and visit you soon.
Where should I send my letters to? Are you still at the temple in Benares?
Yes. Until I find my river I will be at the temple.
At the insistence of the lama, Kim climbed back into the carriage and ordered the driver to take him and his luggage into the school.
Do not weep.
Go up to the gates of learning. Let me see you go.
As the lama walked away, he heard the school gates clang shut; and then he began to cry.
Look after yourself, my disciple.
ST XAVIER'S LUCKNOW

The atmosphere at St. Xavier's suited Kim.
The boys talked about the adventures they went on...
...treks through jungles and encounters with elephants.
Kim learned to read and write English.
His sharp mind thrived when carrying out the tasks presented to him.
But he still yearned for the greasy sweets of the bazaars.
In the backstreets of Lucknow, Kim found the home of an actress. He wanted her to help him with a disguise, so that he could escape from the school.
Some clothing, and perhaps a dye to color my skin, would be of great help.
The actress agreed to help Kim change his appearance. He told her it was to play a joke on a friend, but the truth was that he craved freedom.
With his disguise complete, Kim boarded a train at Lucknow station. In the prickly heat, he took his place in a second class compartment.

The news of Kim's disappearance was reported the next day, by wire, to Colonel Creighton who was in Simla. Mahbub Ali was also in Simla to sell a horse, and he made arrangements to meet with the colonel at Annandale racecourse.
Kim has disappeared. Did you know of this?
Yes, he has gone back to the road for a while.
He sent me a letter before he left, telling me of his intentions.
Read it for yourself. The school has worn him down. He needs time on his own.
He should not go off alone--
But he will be alone when he becomes an agent for us in the Great Game*. He needs to get used to it.
*The struggle between the British and Russian Empires to gain control over Central Asia in the 19th and 20th centuries was known as the Great Game.
Colonel Creighton was beginning to understand just how much potential Kim could have for the British Secret Service. Here was a boy who could outwit those around him and was very independent for his age.
Kim will return. Be patient and let him have some time to himself.

A month later, in the rains of Ambala, Kim found Mahbub Ali on the Kalka road. Mahbub had been delivering horses, and he was not surprised that Kim had managed to track him down.
Is the colonel angry? I don't wish to be beaten.
My hand of friendship has prevented your punishment.
You must be tired. I have a room near the train station.
Come, the landlord will feed us both.
I have assured the colonel's whip will not touch you this time...
...but running away is not good.
I will do what I want. I did not ask to be put there.
If the colonel wants you to be there, then you should be there.
You like me enough to trust my judgement—true?
True. And you should trust me too. The night my lama and I came to you...
...a man searched your things. But I did not give up the letter. Or you.

When you handed me over to Colonel Creighton, I thought you had betrayed me.
Now I think you did me a good turn.
I will stay at the school on one condition...
...that I have complete freedom, without question, when the school is shut.
Ask that of the colonel for me.
I would also like to see my lama again.
I shall ask the colonel if this is possible. Here is some money. Tonight you will sleep among my horse boys at the other end of the station.
Your horse boys will beat me if I arrive without proof of permission.
You will not be beaten as long as you carry this.
Men know my mark from east to west. Now go and get some sleep.

Mahbub's horse boys were camped on a piece of waste ground beside the railway. Kim lay down and closed his eyes, but was soon stirred from his sleep.
If there is such a good price on Mahbub Ali's head, why don't we hire someone to drug him?
No. We will not do that until the Afghan comes to collect his horses...
...and then we will kill him with one bullet.
I must warn Mahbub.
Mahbub Ali, unaware that some men were plotting to kill him, had ridden out to check that Kim was comfortable and keep watch over him.
Mahbub! Some men are waiting here to kill you.
They carry guns, and one of them is the man who searched your things in Lahore.
Go back to my room and wait there.
There are two fakirs crouched outside. I think they are trying to steal some grain from the train carts.
Mahbub decided to report the two men to the British police, whose job it was to protect the train station.
I hope, for their sakes, they are not in possession of a gun when the British find them.
Suspecting that the interests of the railway station were in danger, the British police immediately went to question and search the two fakirs.

Act like thieves and carry guns, will you? Not on my watch, you won't!
Mahbub Ali looked on as the fakirs felt the wrath of the British police.
The British police found their guns! Ho Ha!
Ten good years in jail for them.
The next day, Mahbub Ali took Kim to Simla.
I received word from Colonel Creighton yesterday.
He wants you to stay in Simla, at the home of a man called Mr. Lurgan.
I would rather stay with you, Mahbub.
SIMLA
For the moment, you must do as Colonel Creighton orders. If he tells you to do something, it is for your own good. You must also obey Mr. Lurgan and do what he tells you to do.
Goodbye for now, Kim. This is where the Great Game begins for you.

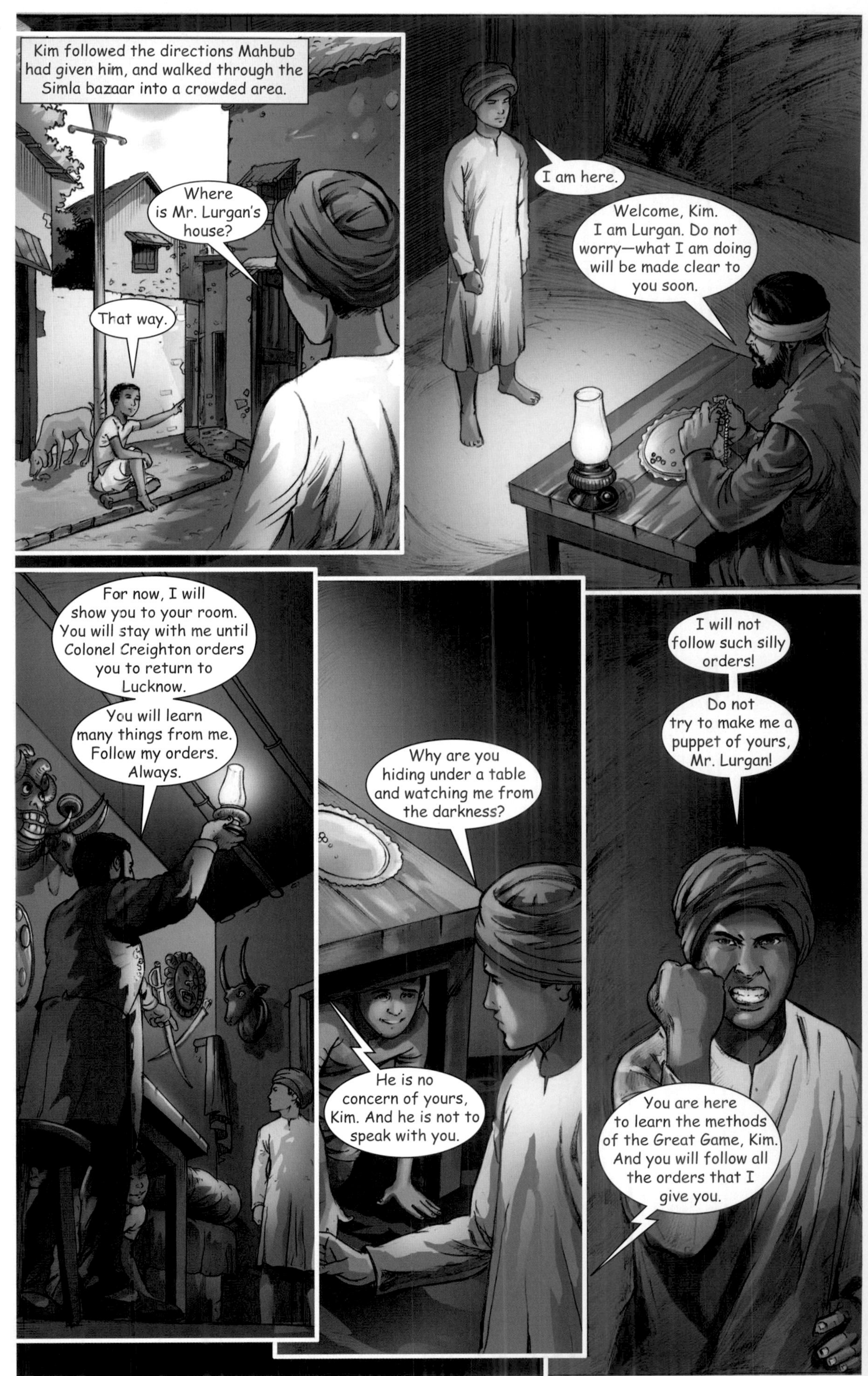
Kim followed the directions Mahbub had given him, and walked through the Simla bazaar into a crowded area.
Where is Mr. Lurgan's house?
That way.
I am here.
Welcome, Kim. I am Lurgan. Do not worry—what I am doing will be made clear to you soon.
For now, I will show you to your room. You will stay with me until Colonel Creighton orders you to return to Lucknow.
You will learn many things from me. Follow my orders. Always.
Why are you hiding under a table and watching me from the darkness?
He is no concern of yours, Kim. And he is not to speak with you.
I will not follow such silly orders!
Do not try to make me a puppet of yours, Mr. Lurgan!
You are here to learn the methods of the Great Game, Kim. And you will follow all the orders that I give you.

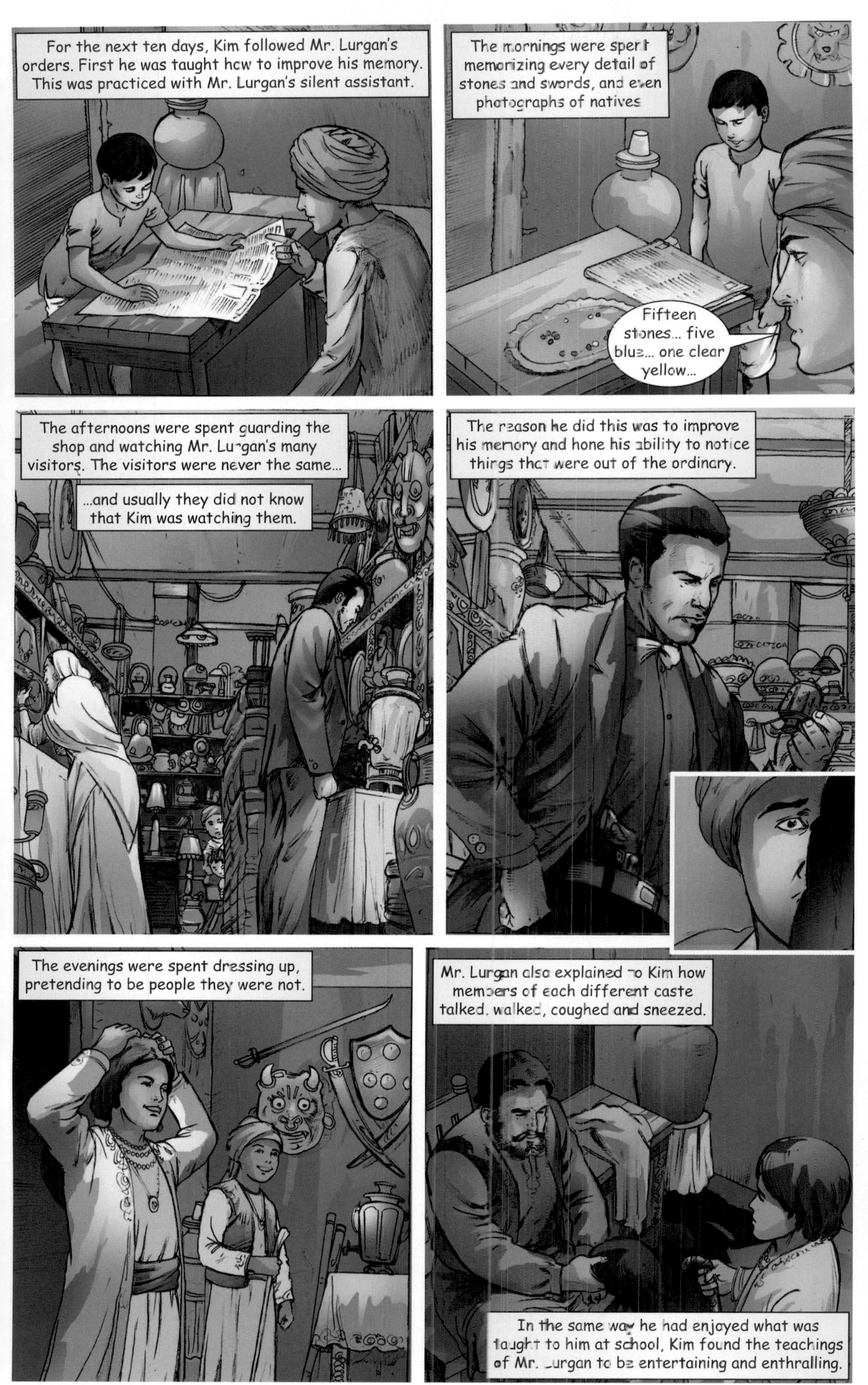
For the next ten days, Kim followed Mr. Lurgan's orders. First he was taught how to improve his memory. This was practiced with Mr. Lurgan's silent assistant.
The mornings were spent memorizing every detail of stones and swords, and even photographs of natives.
Fifteen stones... five blue... one clear yellow...
The afternoons were spent guarding the shop and watching Mr. Lurgan's many visitors. The visitors were never the same...
...and usually they did not know that Kim was watching them.
The reason he did this was to improve his memory and hone his ability to notice things that were out of the ordinary.
The evenings were spent dressing up, pretending to be people they were not.
Mr. Lurgan also explained to Kim how members of each different caste talked, walked, coughed and sneezed.
In the same way he had enjoyed what was taught to him at school, Kim found the teachings of Mr. Lurgan to be entertaining and enthralling.

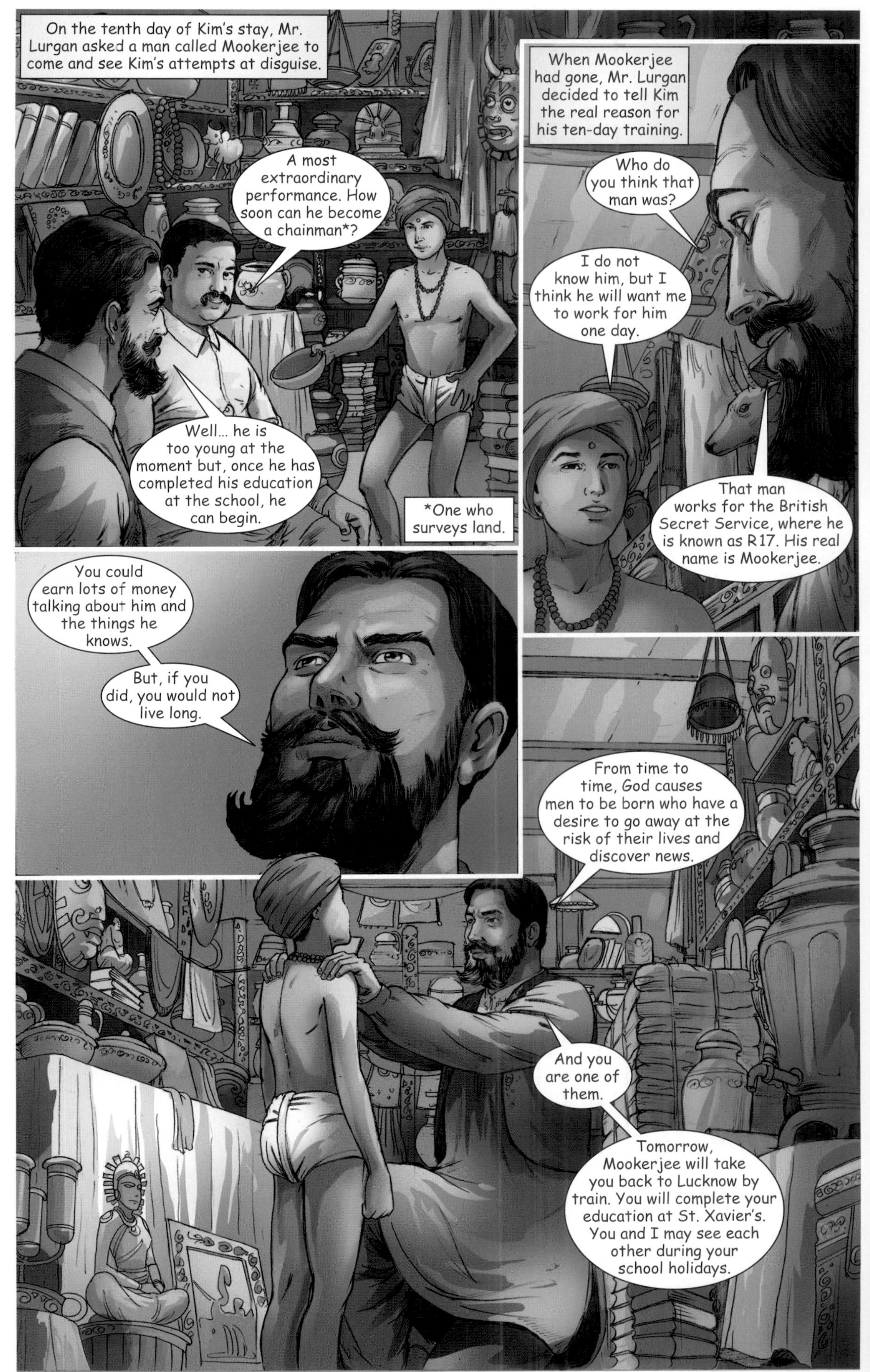
On the tenth day of Kim's stay, Mr. Lurgan asked a man called Mookerjee to come and see Kim's attempts at disguise.
A most extraordinary performance. How soon can he become a chainman*?
Well… he is too young at the moment but, once he has completed his education at the school, he can begin.
*One who surveys land.
When Mookerjee had gone, Mr. Lurgan decided to tell Kim the real reason for his ten-day training.
Who do you think that man was?
I do not know him, but I think he will want me to work for him one day.
That man works for the British Secret Service, where he is known as R17. His real name is Mookerjee.
You could earn lots of money talking about him and the things he knows.
But, if you did, you would not live long.
From time to time, God causes men to be born who have a desire to go away at the risk of their lives and discover news.
And you are one of them.
Tomorrow, Mookerjee will take you back to Lucknow by train. You will complete your education at St. Xavier's. You and I may see each other during your school holidays.

The next day, Kim waited at the train station on the outskirts of Simla. As he left Mr. Lurgan's house, he was reminded to study hard at St. Xavier's.
Mookerjee told Kim that it would be in his best interests to study Latin and French.
KALKA
He was also instructed to learn the precise length of his footsteps. This would allow him to calculate distances in foreign lands.
Remember what I told you today, and take these with you. They are medicines.
Thank you, Mookerjee.
Kim returned to Lucknow, where he attended St. Xavier's and excelled in his studies—most notably in map-making and mathematics.

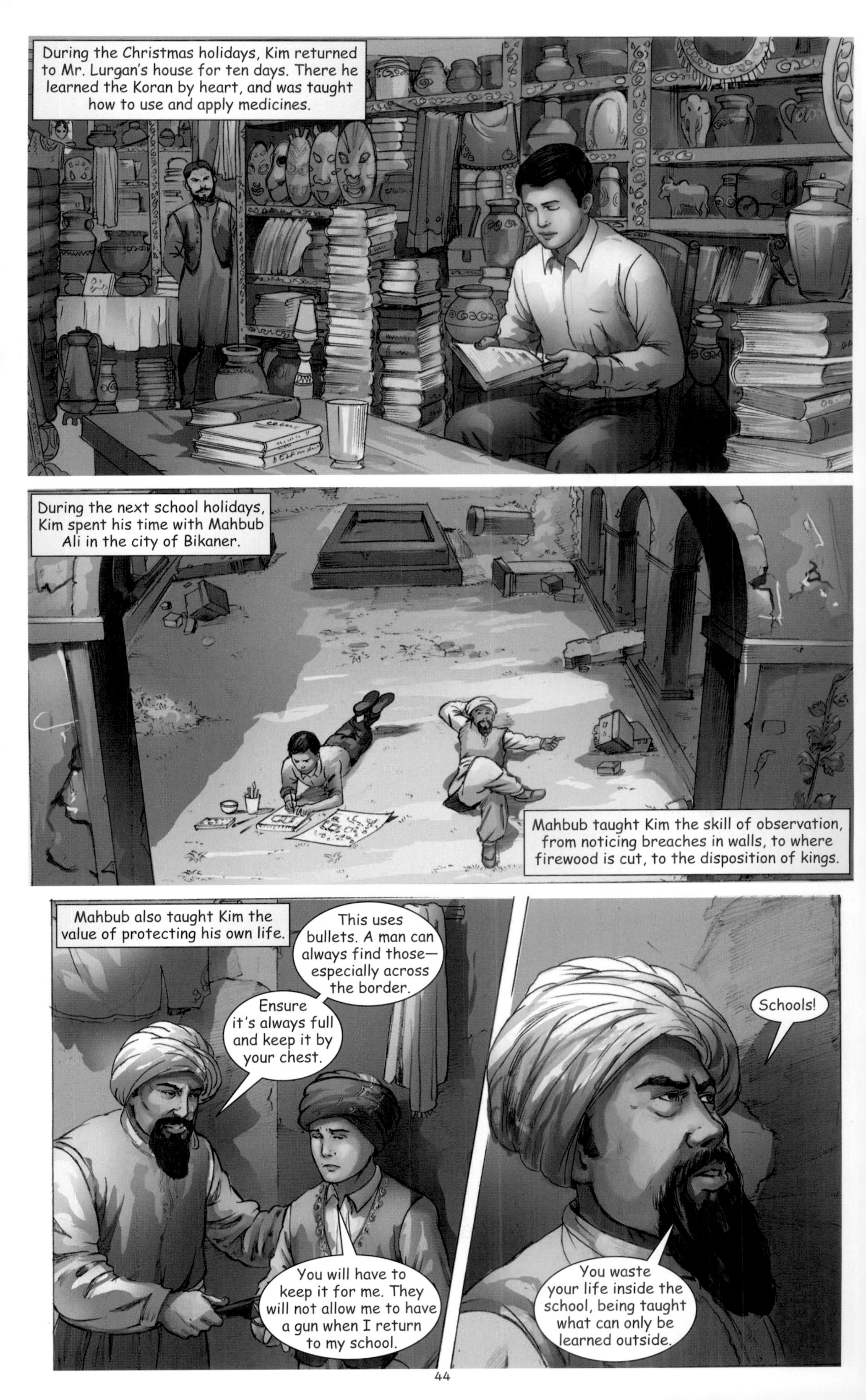
During the Christmas holidays, Kim returned to Mr. Lurgan's house for ten days. There he learned the Koran by heart, and was taught how to use and apply medicines.
During the next school holidays, Kim spent his time with Mahbub Ali in the city of Bikaner.
Mahbub taught Kim the skill of observation, from noticing breaches in walls, to where firewood is cut, to the disposition of kings.
Mahbub also taught Kim the value of protecting his own life.
This uses bullets. A man can always find those—especially across the border.
Ensure it's always full and keep it by your chest.
You will have to keep it for me. They will not allow me to have a gun when I return to my school.
Schools!
You waste your life inside the school, being taught what can only be learned outside.

When Kim returned to school once again, Mahbub Ali and Colonel Creighton met at the house of Mr. Lurgan to discuss Kim's future.
Kim must leave his school. He should be working for the Secret Service now!
THUD
But he is so young, Mahbub—he has only just turned sixteen.
By the time I was fifteen years old, I had already shot a man!
Mahbub is right, Colonel Creighton. Kim is strong enough now. He is wasted at that school.
Colonel Creighton could not ignore the advice of both Mr. Lurgan and Mahbub.
Perhaps you are right. But there is no work for him to do at the moment. Don't worry, he will work for the British Secret Service soon enough.
Perhaps Kim should be allowed to spend some time traveling with the lama?
Yes, he can travel with the lama for the next six months, unless some work arises that is suitable for him.
Colonel Creighton knew that Kim would be safe with the lama. However, he asked Mahbub to prepare Kim for the Great Game, just in case.
Before he sets off with the lama, take him to Hureefa.

Huneefa was a spiritualist who lived in Lucknow.
I am taking you to a woman who will cast a spell that will protect you from danger.
You are far too pale, Kim. Huneefa has a magic dye that will not fade after a week or even a month.
As a superstitious man, Mahbub Ali asked Huneefa to perform a ritual which would give Kim full protection from danger.
AAAIIIIEEEEAAIIIEEEII
Ah, Mookerjee, you have come. Take Kim to the station so that he may travel to see his lama.
Make sure the lama does not take him to a place we cannot find.

The ceremony that Huneefa performed left Kim tired and exhausted. He was woken by Mookerjee who was eager to tell him more secrets of the British Secret Service.
If you find yourself in a tight spot out there...
...say 'I am son of the charm.'
It means you might be a member of a secret society.
Natives will think before killing you, giving you an extra chance for life.
This amulet, which we've placed around your neck, is given to everyone in our department.
We will be in disguises out there. This is the only way you will identify me or anyone else.
If someone asks you if you want to buy precious stones...
...or if they mention turquoise, curry or castes...
...you should respond by saying, 'there is no caste when men go to look for curry.'
Those words are the code that will identify someone as belonging to the British Secret Service.
At Lucknow train station, Kim bought a ticket to take him to Benares. He felt happy at the thought of finally rejoining his lama in the search for the river.

When he arrived in Benares, Kim went straight to the temple.
I am the disciple to a holy man here. Please tell him Kim has arrived.
If you know a holy man here, please tell him to cure my son. I beg you!
Please help my child, Holy One! He has a terrible fever.
We shall try to help your son.
He is weak and cannot stand up.
It is no more than a fever. He is not well fed.
I have something for him.
What! Have they made you a healer?
Boil three of the brown pills in milk, and three in water. Give him the white pill when he wakes up.
The healing skills that Kim had learned from Mr. Lurgan delighted the lama.
To heal the sick is to acquire merit.
That was wisely done, Kim.
I was made wise by you, Holy One.

The lama led Kim to his living quarters inside the temple. He wanted to show Kim his drawing of the Wheel of Life.
Holy One, I will soon work for Colonel Creighton. But for the moment, I want to follow you in your search for the river.
So you shall, Kim. We will head north together, but first I want to show you my drawing.
The lama explained to Kim that he was still no closer to understanding where the River of Enlightenment was. However, he was convinced that, if they traveled together, it was surely their destiny to find it.
What does this drawing signify, Holy One?
We all have a destiny and a place to go where we must go. We will use the Wheel of Life to help us understand our journey and ourselves.
The next morning, while waiting at Benares station for a train to the north, Kim and the lama came across the man whose son Kim's medicine had saved.
I am taking my son back to his mother in Delhi. Thank you so much. Do you mind if I travel with you?
Of course not. Please join us.
A man, who looked as if he had been badly beaten, then entered the train carriage. He gave an explanation for his cuts and bruises, but Kim did not believe his story.
What happened? Are you badly hurt?
A cart turned over and nearly killed me.
He wears an amulet like mine!
The man had also noticed that Kim wore a similar amulet to his.

Besides the harm the cart did to me, I also lost a full dish of curry.
I was not a son of the charm that day.
The man had chosen to reveal himself as a member of the British Secret Service. He had recited part of the code which Mookerjee had taught to Kim.
You talk about curry, but what do you think about caste?
There is no caste when men go to look for curry.
When the man was satisfied that Kim was an agent in training, he began to explain why he was traveling to Delhi.
What really happened to you?
I stole a letter from a king. I managed to hide it in Chittor, but I was captured and badly beaten by his guards.
I then managed to escape, but I am now a wanted man.
I have been chased from the south to the north.
I am known in the Service as E.23.
E.23 knew that entering Delhi could either mean success or death.
When I reach Delhi, I will try to send a message to Simla about the letter I have hidden. However, if I am caught, I will be killed before I get the chance.

From what Mr. Lurgan had taught Kim, he knew there was a way that E. 23 could avoid being captured in Delhi.
I am carrying dyes and opium. I will use them to change your appearance.
I will make you into a yellow sadhu.
Using the dye to change E. 23's skin color, and offering him opium to redden the color of his eyes, Kim began to transform him.
Hurry! We must disguise you before the train reaches Delhi.
The onlookers could only express amazement as Kim changed E. 23 beyond recognition.
What magic is this? We are traveling with warlocks!
You will tell no one of this!
Please do not curse my household. I saw nothing! I heard nothing!
Kim knew that fear of the unknown would keep the witnesses silent.
Delhi Train Station.
That young policeman has my description on that piece of paper! They will search every carriage
The king, who E. 23 had stolen the letter from, had told the British police—who knew nothing about the Secret Service—that E. 23 had committed murders and should be arrested on sight.

It seemed that E. 23 was right; the British police began to search the train, carriage by carriage.
None of them matches the description of the murderer. Come on, let's go.
I see a man out there who is in the Secret Service. I must let him know I have succeeded in obtaining the letter.
I saved your life just now, but you want to risk it again?
Have faith in me. My work must not be left unfinished.
Kim was amazed that E. 23 had turned his emotions from fear of death to fear of failure.
Ouch! The blue parrots fly east in winter, my brother.
You drunken idiot! Get back in your carriage before I beat you.
My friend out there in the crowd heard my code words. He will tell the others I have succeeded.
He is the greatest agent in the whole of the British Secret Service. I will tell him how you have helped me.
I predict you will be in the Great Game longer than I will be, my friend. Remember, we of the Great Game are beyond protection.
It suddenly dawned on Kim that the role he was being groomed for was of great risk to those who performed it.

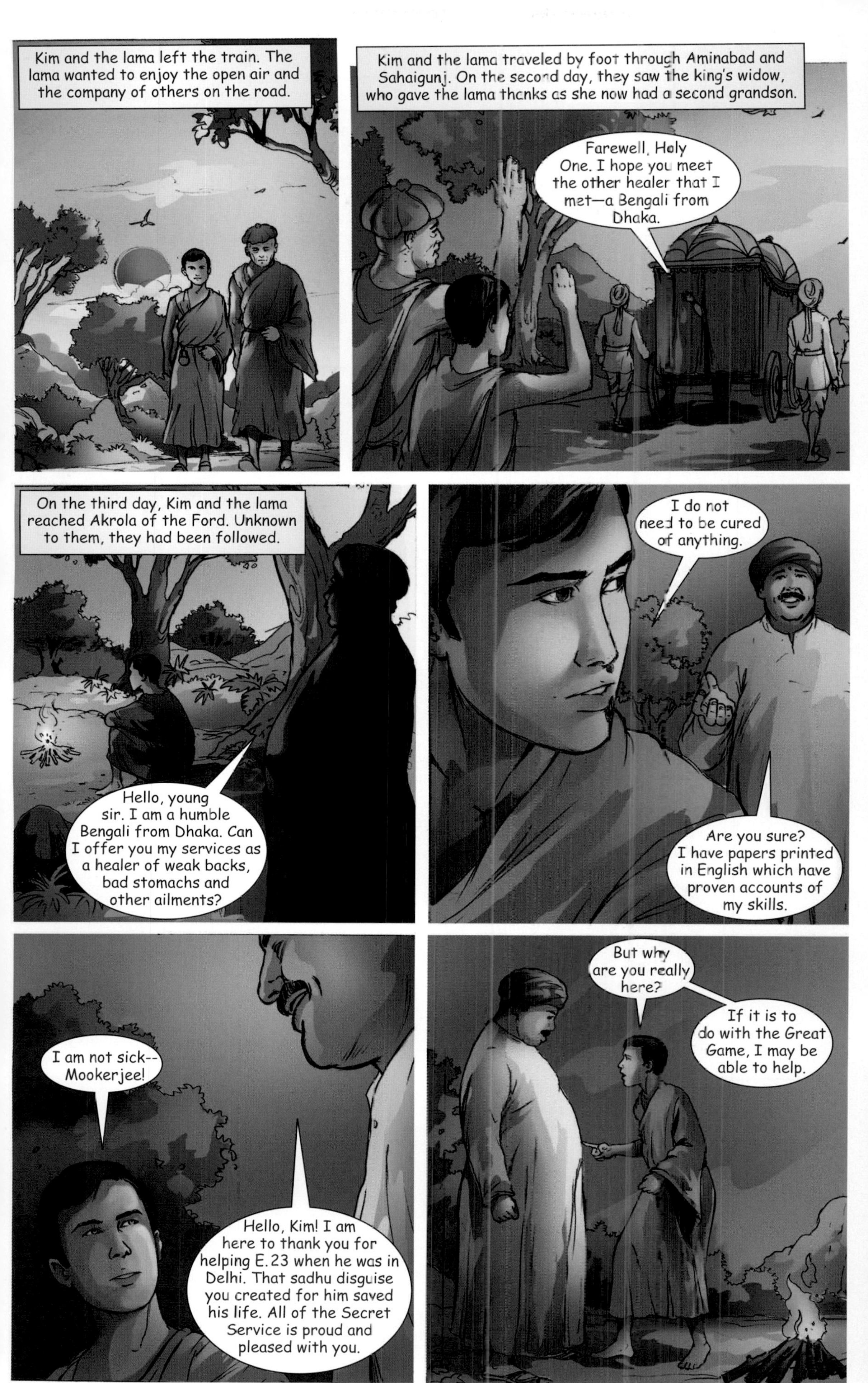
Kim and the lama left the train. The lama wanted to enjoy the open air and the company of others on the road.
Kim and the lama traveled by foot through Aminabad and Sahaigunj. On the second day, they saw the king's widow, who gave the lama thanks as she now had a second grandson.
Farewell, Holy One. I hope you meet the other healer that I met—a Bengali from Dhaka.
On the third day, Kim and the lama reached Akrola of the Ford. Unknown to them, they had been followed.
Hello, young sir. I am a humble Bengali from Dhaka. Can I offer you my services as a healer of weak backs, bad stomachs and other ailments?
I do not need to be cured of anything.
Are you sure? I have papers printed in English which have proven accounts of my skills.
I am not sick-- Mookerjee!
Hello, Kim! I am here to thank you for helping E.23 when he was in Delhi. That sadhu disguise you created for him saved his life. All of the Secret Service is proud and pleased with you.
But why are you really here?
If it is to do with the Great Game, I may be able to help.

Later that night, Mookerjee decided to tell Kim more about the Great Game and those who played it.
Kim, do you remember the message you delivered to Colonel Creighton three years ago? It concerned the pedigree of a white stallion.
I remember the truth of it was that it concerned a war. Please tell me all the details.
Mookerjee explained to Kim that the message had warned Colonel Creighton of five kings who were preparing to wage a war. The British were able to prepare an army, which prevented the war from occurring.
At that time, the British government believed that the kings were frightened and would not attempt to start another war.
In an attempt to make peace with the kings, the British government agreed to build new roads in the hills for two of them.
The two kings agreed that the new roads would be guarded to stop anyone coming in from the north.
However, it became apparent that the kings had asked for the roads so they could supply a footpath to the enemies of the British—the Russians.
The Russians had befriended the kings with gifts and promises of wealth. However, the Russians wanted the roads so that their armies could travel into India.
Now two Russians were approaching from the north. They were carrying levels, chains and compasses in order to decide where their armies could erect forts. The British Secret Service had sent Mookerjee to meet them.

These two Russians are very ruthless.
They will do whatever it takes to complete their mission. I will have to be careful when dealing with them.
Now, I must be on my way. I would like you to try and keep in touch with me. If you do, I will include it in my report—it would be a great feather in your cap.
Think it over.
Now Kim felt his opinions and decisions were beginning to be treated with respect. He was truly a player in the Great Game.
The next morning, Kim tried to convince the lama to keep traveling north, so that he could follow Mookerjee. He had said he would only be four or five miles ahead of them.
Go north you say?
Why not? We will avoid the heat and walk in the hills.
You say it is our destiny to find the River of Enlightenment...
...if that is true, then we will find our river, no matter what.
With the Himalayas close by, the lama agreed that they should continue north. However, Kim would come to regret avoiding the heat.

These are only the lower hills, my disciple. We will not feel the cold until we come to the true Himalayas.
I am feeling the cold already, Holy One.
It's too c-cold.
We cannot always delight in warm beds and rich food, Kim.
The lama was surprised that anyone would object to the cold temperature, which he felt had kept him young.
Meanwhile, Mookerjee had been tracking the two Russians.
As he had expected, they came through the Chini Valley, which is where he found them camped.
Mookerjee introduced himself to the Russians, and learned that their guide had fallen sick and so could no longer travel with them.
When he offered his services as a guide, the Russians accepted, unaware of his real intentions.
The Russians asked Mookerjee to take them to Simla. He agreed, but delayed them for a while to allow Kim to catch up.
That man over there is a holy man.
What is he doing?
He is reading a holy picture, a kind of map.
These men are the Russians I spoke of. I have word that they are carrying a letter of great importance.
They are guarding that letter very carefully.

No! It's not for sale. Don't you understand, it's--
Tell the holy man I want the map now!
RRIIIPP
Behind Kim and Mookerjee, a group of Buddhist railway workers looked on in horror as the lama's drawing was destroyed.
What have you done!
Do you see this, Kim? These Russians are vicious and mean!
You must not hit a holy man!
No!
I said I want the map!
SMAK!
Uggghhhhhh!
Seeing the lama struck, Kim launched himself at the attacker like an animal.
Argggghhh!
The temper which had made Kim's father such a good soldier now awakened in Kim.

You should not have hit him like that. You shall pay for it!
Crazy boy!
Back away or I will shoot you like dogs!
They have beaten a holy man. Sacrilege!
Although one of the Russians carried a handgun, it did him little good when faced with the onslaught that came from the railway workers.
Stop that!
THUD!
Come, Holy One. We will help you.
Mookerjee did his best to stop the Russian from making the situation any worse than it already was.
The railway workers are taking our bags and rifles!
Please sir, stop shooting! I will get your things back for you.
On the other side of the hill, Mookerjee found that Kim was still beating the other Russian.
Kim! Stop beating him. The railway workers have the Russians' bags.
The papers are in the bags. Go and get them, Kim.
We must stop the railway workers!
Shooting at them is not going to get you your things back. We need to look after your friend for now. He is badly hurt.

Although he had been struck, the lama was able to walk and wanted to continue on the journey to find the river.
Did they hurt you, my disciple?
No, and you?
I am unhurt. Come, Kim, we will travel with these men to Shamlegh.
We will have justice first. The man who struck the lama must be punished!
The Russian who had been beaten by Kim felt unwell and could not travel any further. Mookerjee insisted he and his companion stay at the bottom of the hill and rest.
You hit a holy man! You should consider yourselves lucky to be alive.
The railway workers had not forgiven the Russians for their actions, and were at the top of the hill planning an attack.
We have their guns, and they struck the lama.
Let us go down there and kill them!
After striking a holy man, the Russians were chartless, foodless and gunless. It seems their Great Game had collapsed due to their stupidity.
ZZZZZZZ
ZZZZZZZ
Let them go. It is not worth it.
Do you wish to be reborn as a rat or a snake?
The lama convinced the railway workers not to kill the Russians, but they insisted on firing one shot to frighten them away.
BANG!
Look! Up there in the trees!
They're going to kill us. We must leave now!

Mookerjee led the Russians away to safety. Meanwhile, the railway workers insisted that Kim and the lama stay with them for the night, under their protection.
It may be a curse. Give it to me and I will ensure it causes us no harm.
We will divide the Russians' things amongst ourselves. What does this letter say?
We will give it to you when we reach Shamlegh.
The lama, unable to sleep, climbed to the top of a hill which looked down on Shamlegh. He wanted to give himself time to think.
Holy One, are you alright?
No. I feel guilt, Kim.
When that man struck me, I wanted to tell the railway workers to kill him.
I managed to overcome my desire for revenge. In the future, I must be passionless. You must learn that lesson too, my disciple.
I am sorry that I do not agree with you at this moment. I am glad that I hurt the man who struck you.
Be well, Holy One.
The lama returned to the camp to sleep. For a time, Kim thought about what he had said; he did not understand how anyone could be passionless when attacked.

When Kim and the lama woke the next morning, the railway workers had already gone. When they reached Shamlegh, a woman asked Kim to enter her home.
I am known as the Woman of Shamlegh. A group of railway workers asked me to give this to a boy called Kim. That must be you.
The Woman of Shamlegh gave Kim and the lama a meal, after which Kim began to search the Russians' things.
What are you looking for, Kim?
It is none of your concern. You would be better off to look away.
A man was here yesterday. He also mentioned you—his name was Mookerjee.
After a thorough search, Kim found survey instruments, books, diaries, letters, maps and correspondence.
Yes, I know that man. I will ask you to communicate with him for me soon. I will make him very happy when I see him.
I have all that I need. The rest is just inconvenient evidence.
Kim went to destroy the remaining items belonging to the Russians. The lama had stayed behind at the Woman of Shamlegh's house—their lengthy journey had exhausted him.
Now you will carry word to the man known as Mookerjee. You shall take a letter to him for me.
Yes, Kim. He is in the forest somewhere nearby.
The lama's exhaustion became sickness and he could not leave his bed. Kim sent the Woman of Shamlegh to find Mookerjee and give him the news.
I am at Shamlegh. The old man is sick. Tell me what to do.

Mookerjee sent a message to Kim through the Woman of Shamlegh. He said he was unable to help the lama as he could not leave the Russians alone. But, once he had taken them to Simla, he would join Kim.
So Mookerjee and these Russians are still in the forest here?
Yes... tell the villagers to feed them and leave them in peace.
We must get them quietly away from this valley.
When Kim went back to the Woman of Shamlegh's house, he found the lama wandering outside. He looked very sick.
Do not worry about me, Kim. I have seen the error of my ways. This is what has made me sick.
The lama told Kim of a time when he and some other monks had strayed from the way of non-violence and had fought over the rule of a valley. Another monk had attacked him and struck him hard on his head.
The Russian's blow landed on the scar I have on my head. This is a reminder that I must avoid all violent thoughts.
I forgot my search for the river and had violent thoughts which have darkened my soul. I must find the river now. Come, Kim, we must leave immediately.

Why is he not resting? He is still sick.
I know, but he insists that we both leave now.
You will not get far. He can barely walk.
As hard as he tried, the lama could go no further. He toppled over and the Woman of Shamlegh told Kim what he already knew.
We must continue our search for the River of Enlightenment.
He cannot travel, unless you intend to carry him on your shoulders.
At the insistence of the Woman of Shamlegh, Kim allowed two of her brothers to carry the lama on a stretcher. They would head south-east out of Shamlegh, resuming their quest for the River of Enlightenment.
The bag too. Carry it all.
Here is some money.
You might need it.
Thank you.
Goodbye, my dear.

The next morning, Mookerjee waved goodbye to the two Russians. He took them to the borders of Nahan, and they thanked him for saving them from the wrath of the railway workers.
They had no clue that he was an agent of the British Secret Service and that their private documents would soon be handed to Colonel Creighton.
Once Mookerjee saw the Russians disappear over the horizon, he began to search for Kim.
I saw a boy traveling with a lama. They were going in that direction.
The brothers of the Woman of Shamlegh carried the lama through Mussoorie to a house on the edge of the Doon valley. Kim was sure the owner of the house would help him.
I am looking for a king's widow who lives here. May I speak with her?
I have brought you to the house of the king's widow. She will help us, and you will be well soon.
Try to rest and do not worry. We will find the River of Enlightenment.
Come! Bring him in as quick as you can.
Try to relax. The lama will be well. You also need rest.
The king's widow immediately attended to Kim and the lama.

Kim, aching in every bone from exhaustion, was taken to a bedroom to rest.
I must have a locked box for the holy one. It is for his prayers.
One shall be brought and you will have the key. But now you need rest. Help him onto the bed.
Although Kim still felt tired after sleeping for a while, he knew he had to organize the items taken from the Russians.
Kim knew that Mookerjee would soon find him, and that the items needed to be in order for Colonel Creighton. His sense of duty outweighed his need to rest.
You are very devoted to the lama. I was wrong to doubt you before.
I think your devotion has made you ill.
After hearing the words of the king's widow, Kim fell into a deep sleep and remained there for a week.
ZZZZZZZ
All that week, the king's widow kept a close watch on Kim. When he arose, her face was the first he saw.
Where is the lama? Is he better?
He fell into a brook while out walking, but he is fine now.
The Bengali healer is here too.
He asked about you and the lama.
Please send the healer to me.
Kim had been right all along. Mookerjee, the British Secret Service's best agent, had found him with relative ease.

Young Mr O'Hara! I am jolly glad to see you. What do you think of my disguise?
Here. Take the key and see for yourself.
It suits you, Mookerjee. You will be jolly glad with the contents of this box. It contains the Russians' papers and maps!
Ha Ha! A letter from King Hilas! I shall take these back to Colonel Creighton immediately.
The Russians told me they had lost eight months' work.
Then they gave me a letter praising the help I gave them. Ha Ha! Is that not a great joke?
For guiding the Russians to safety, Mookerjee had not only been thanked by them, but they had also left evidence that the five kings were conspiring with the Russians against the British.
Mr. Lurgan and the department are all very proud of you, Kim—especially Mahbub Ali.
He has come here to see you, and I made him bring all his men with him. He wasn't too happy about that.
Have you seen my holy one?
Yes, he nearly drowned. It was I who pulled him out of the brook.
Ha Ha! He finally found his river.
Kim and the lama had searched for the River of Enlightenment. The fact that the lama had unwittingly stumbled into water made Kim laugh at the irony.
Despite the successes and victories, Kim felt like his soul was out of step with its surroundings.
I am Kim. Who is Kim? Who am I really?
Was Kim to travel with the lama? Or join the Great Game permanently? It was a decision he felt was out of his hands.

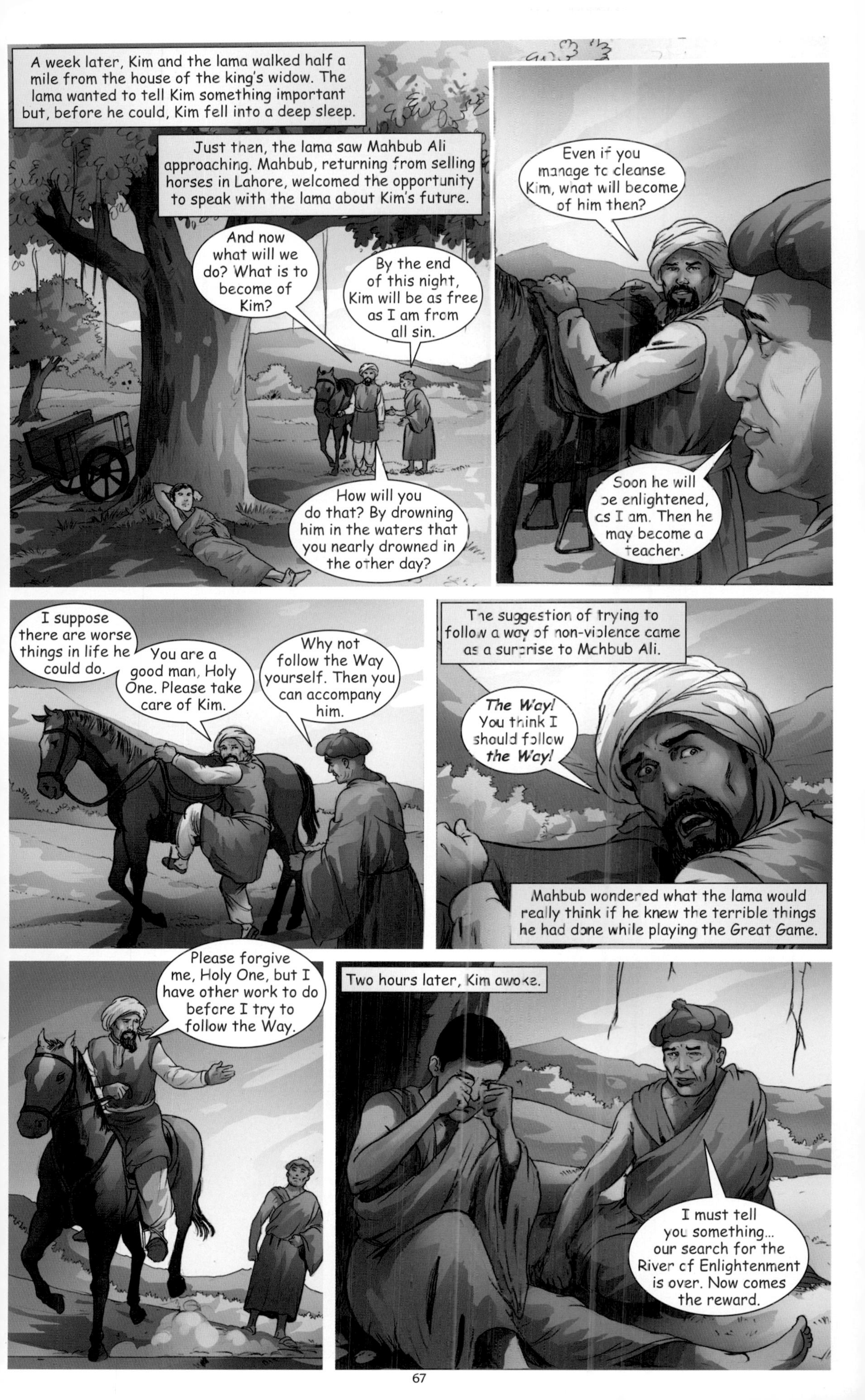

A week later, Kim and the lama walked half a mile from the house of the king's widow. The lama wanted to tell Kim something important but, before he could, Kim fell into a deep sleep.
Just then, the lama saw Mahbub Ali approaching. Mahbub, returning from selling horses in Lahore, welcomed the opportunity to speak with the lama about Kim's future.
And now what will we do? What is to become of Kim?
By the end of this night, Kim will be as free as I am from all sin.
How will you do that? By drowning him in the waters that you nearly drowned in the other day?
Even if you manage to cleanse Kim, what will become of him then?
Soon he will be enlightened, as I am. Then he may become a teacher.
I suppose there are worse things in life he could do.
You are a good man, Holy One. Please take care of Kim.
Why not follow the Way yourself. Then you can accompany him.
The suggestion of trying to follow a way of non-violence came as a surprise to Mahbub Ali.
The Way! You think I should follow *the Way!*
Mahbub wondered what the lama would really think if he knew the terrible things he had done while playing the Great Game.
Please forgive me, Holy One, but I have other work to do before I try to follow the Way.
Two hours later, Kim awoke.
I must tell you something... our search for the River of Enlightenment is over. Now comes the reward.

The time had come for the lama to share his experience of enlightenment with Kim.
When we were among the hills, I relied on your strength to save me. The effort you gave made you unwell.
When we arrived at the house of the king's widow, I took no food and drank no water. Instead, I meditated. I hoped I would soon see the way, but I did not.
It was only when I fell into the brook that I asked myself what would happen to you if I died. Who would show you the Way, and what path would you take?
The water cleansed me from my sins. My soul was purified because I thought of your life, and I have acquired enlightenment for that. One must think of others at all times, and avoid all violent actions and thoughts. That is the way life should be lived.
The lama then smiled, as a man does when he wins salvation for himself and his friend.

Mark Twain

JOAN OF ARC

Adapted by Tony DiGerolamo

Illustrated by Rajesh Nagulakonda

Uniting a beleaguered nation, a young girl named Joan leads it to improbable victories. A story that will both inform and inspire.

Joan of Arc was gifted with visions instructing her to liberate France from the armies of the English. As a young woman she defied friends, family, and even members of the government in her attempts to free the French.

By the strength of her personality and her ability to foretell the future, Joan convinced the King of France to grant her an armed force. In return, she led her small band of followers to take on and defeat the might of the English. Her conviction ensured her a place at the forefront of France's military history.

During her adventures, Joan of Arc inspired unlikely allies to join her, faced danger unflinchingly, planned battle-winning strategies and had the insight to motivate a nation. All that stood between Joan and her visions becoming reality were the treacherous actions of bureaucrats, and a King unable to think for himself.

From Mark Twain, the writer of *The Adventures of Tom Sawyer* and *The Adventures of Huckleberry Finn* (also published by Campfire), comes an engaging tale of friendship, courage, conviction, and treachery.

www.campfire.co.in

SPIES AND THE ART OF SPYING

TRAINING

Do you want to be a good spy? Then you must excel at Kim's Game, named after an exercise Kim goes through during his training as a spy. In its most simple form, 10 or 15 objects are put on a tray that is shown to a person for a minute. The tray is then covered and the person is asked to remember all the different objects. The greater the number of objects remembered, the better! It greatly tests and develops a person's observation and memory skills—skills essential for a good spy!

SPYING TECHNIQUES

DEAD DROP OR DEAD LETTER BOX

A dead drop, or dead letter box, is a location which is used to secretly pass things between two spies or agents. It involves locations and signals agreed on beforehand. The dead drop could be the space behind a loose brick in a wall, a hollowed book or a hole in a tree. A mark on a wall, a newspaper on a bench or even a potted plant at a window—the most ordinary of everyday objects—can all serve as signals of the drop.

CONCEALMENT DEVICES

Concealment devices are used to hide important information or objects. They are made from ordinary items such as a candle, a can, or even something as small as a coin—objects that would not arouse any suspicion. A hollow candle looks like a large ordinary candle, but has enough space to conceal an object or a piece of paper. There have been instances of hollowed-out coins or teeth being used by spies for concealing suicide pills.

STEGANOGRAPHY

Steganography is the science of writing hidden messages. The aim is to make sure that no one, apart from the sender and recipient, even realizes that a message exists. The use of photographically produced microdots (text or images reduced to the size of a tiny dot), as well as messages in invisible inks, was common during World War II. Another example of the use of steganography was by Velvalee Dickinson (known as the Doll Woman), a spy for the Japanese living in America during World War II. She was a dealer in dolls and sent secret messages containing information about the US Naval forces to the Japanese in letters discussing her dolls!

DID YOU KNOW?

Cher Ami was a homing pigeon which carried important messages during World War I and helped save the lives of more than a hundred soldiers of the US Army Signal Corps in France. He became quite a hero after the war and was awarded many medals for his bravery!

SPYING DURING WARTIME

Wartime sees the use of new methods and gadgets by secret agents with the aim to gather as much information as possible about the enemy:

U-2 SPY PLANE

The Lockheed U-2, also known as the Dragon Lady, is a plane used by the US Air Force, which was previously flown by the Central Intelligence Agency (CIA). It has long glider-like wings and can fly at very high altitudes. This makes it difficult for enemy radars to detect its presence. Fitted with sensors and cameras, it is an ideal spy plane.

A famous incident that involved this aircraft occurred during the Cold War (the state of tension and rivalry between the US and the former Soviet Union). On May 1, 1960, an American U-2 spy plane was shot down over the Soviet Union. The American government denied the plane's objective at the beginning. But, later, when evidence was gathered by the Soviet Union from the remains of the plane and the surviving pilot, it accepted that the plane was a surveillance aircraft.

DOUBLE AGENT

A double agent is someone who pretends to work for one side, but actually works for the other. During World War II, the British used many double agents to fool the Germans about what the Allies were up to. Juan Pujol Garcia was one of Britain's top secret agents in World War II. Codenamed Garbo, he became a double agent. He pretended to work for the Germans, while actually working for the British, and played a vital role in tricking the Germans at crucial points during the war. Interestingly, he received military decorations from both sides—an Iron Cross from the Germans and a Member of the Order of the British Empire badge, for his services, from the British!

DID YOU KNOW?

- In 1945, the Soviet Union presented the American Embassy in Moscow with a wooden reproduction of the Great Seal of the United States. It hung in the ambassador's office for seven years before a listening device, or a bug, was discovered in it in 1952!
- It is believed that robobugs are being developed by the US army. They consist of electronic flies, spiders, and other insects. They will be used to gather information undetected and to scuttle into areas too dangerous for humans!

...BLE FROM CAMPFIRE GRAPHIC NOVELS